Chalk and Cheese

PETERS

FRASER
&
DUNLOP

5th⋅⋅⋅⋅⋅⋅⋅⋅⋅⋅⋅⋅
CHELSEA HA⋅⋅⋅⋅⋅
LONDON SW10 0XF

AGENT: RC
ROYALTY SHEET Nº:
PUBLICATION DATE:
CATEGORY:

PETERS FRASER & DUNLOP

PLEASE RETURN TO

503/4 THE CHAMBERS

CHELSEA HARBOUR · LONDON SW10 0XF

TELEPHONE: 0171 - 344 1010

FAX 0171 - 352 7356 · 0171 - 351 1756

Chalk and Cheese

Adèle Geras

Illustrated by
Adriano Gon

CORGI PUPS

For Suzanne

Series Reading Consultant: Prue Goodwin
Reading and Language Information Centre,
University of Reading

CHALK AND CHEESE
A CORGI PUPS BOOK : 0 552 529710
First publication in Great Britain

PRINTING HISTORY
Corgi Pups edition published 1996

Copyright © 1996 by Adèle Geras
Illustration copyright © 1996 by Adriano Gon

The right of Adèle Geras to be identified as the author
of this work has been asserted in accordance with the
Copyright, Designs and Patents Act 1988.

Condition of Sale
This book is sold subject to the condition that it shall not, by way of trade
or otherwise, be lent, re-sold, hired out or otherwise circulated without the
publisher's prior consent in any form of binding or cover other than that in
which it is published and without a similar condition including this
condition being imposed on the subsequent purchaser.

Set in Bembo Schoolbook

Corgi Pups Books are published by Transworld Publishers Ltd,
61–63 Uxbridge Road, Ealing, London W5 5SA,
in Australia by Transworld Publishers (Australia) Pty Ltd,
15–25 Helles Avenue, Moorebank, NSW 2170
and in New Zealand by Transworld Publishers (NZ) Ltd,
3 William Pickering Drive, Albany, Auckland.

Printed and bound in Great Britain by
Cox & Wyman Ltd, Reading, Berkshire.

Contents

Chapter One

"Oh, Mum," Lily moaned. "Do I have to?"

"Yes," said Mum. "You *do* have to. I've got to be out this afternoon and I don't want you here all by yourself. After school, you'll go to ballet class with your sister and then you're both going home with Michelle for tea at her house. I'll come and fetch you at half past six."

"But Jo loves going to ballet," said Lily, "and I hate it. I'll be bored." She groaned and made a face.

Lily went on groaning and making faces on the way to St James's Church Hall after school. That was where Miss Warne's dancing class was held every week. Jo longed for Tuesdays. She loved wearing her pink satin ballet shoes and pink leotard.

"It's not fair," Lily said as they walked along. "I want to ride. Why can't I have the lessons I'd like?"

"Because," said Jo, "we live so far away from any riding stables, right in the middle of a big city.

You could come to ballet like
me."

"No, I couldn't," said Lily.
"Ballet is soppy."

"It isn't," said Jo.

"It is," said Lily.

"We've got four boys in our
class," said Jo.

"Then *they're* soppy," said Lily.
When she got home, she
thought, she would get on the
rocking-horse and pretend to be
a cowboy.

"Stop arguing," said Jo. "Come into the cloakroom and wait while I change."

The four boys in the class got ready in a little room at the back of the hall. The cloakroom was full of girls, chattering and giggling. Some of them had brought their ballet things in small suitcases. They hung their school clothes on the pegs. Some of the coats and cardigans fell on the floor, but nobody noticed. They were too busy.

They twisted their
hair into tidy buns.

They tied the buns up in hairnets.

They put on pink ballet shoes.

They did up the satin ribbons with neat bows.

Then they fluttered into the hall.

They look like flamingoes,
thought Lily. Flamingoes were
pink birds with long, black,
skinny legs. Lily had seen them
on TV.

Miss Warne was very tall and thin. First she made the children line up and do exercises. A lady in a red cardigan was playing the piano. The music went *plink-plonk-plink* and the floor squeaked. After a while, Miss Warne said:

"Now, children, please sit down and listen. As you know, it will soon be time for our Christmas Display, and this year we're going to do a dance based on a scene from a very famous ballet called *The Nutcracker*. The story is about

a little girl called Clara. She gets a
magic nutcracker for Christmas,
in the shape of a man. During the
night, the Nutcracker comes to
life, then he and Clara have a
battle with an army of mice.
Clara throws her slipper at the
Mouse King and the mice run
away." She smiled. "Some of you
are going to be mice in a special
dance I've arranged. Listen
carefully for your names."

Jo was chosen to be a mouse,
and Lily could see from her face
how happy she was.

Chapter Two

Jo thought being a mouse in the dancing display was the best thing that had ever happened to her.

Even though Jo and Lily were sisters, they were very different.

"I wish *my* name was Jo," Lily used to say. "I don't like having the same name as a flower. 'Jo' could be a boy's name."

"My real name is Joanne," said Jo. "*That* couldn't be a boy's name."

Jo and Lily were like chalk and cheese. Jo was nine and small and dainty; Lily was seven, but tall for her age. They could have worn the same clothes if they'd wanted to, but Jo liked the colour pink, and Lily didn't. Jo liked frilly blouses and flowered dresses and pretty ankle socks trimmed with lace. Lily hated everything except jeans and dungarees, worn with a T-shirt in the summer and a jumper in the winter. Jo's shoes were black and shiny, and Lily thought they looked like dolls' shoes. Lily wore trainers with red and silver flashes on the heels. Whenever the sisters played together, they argued about what to do.

"Pirates!" Lily shouted.

"Tea parties!" said Jo.

"Tarzan!" Lily suggested.

"Mothers and babies," said Jo.

Mostly they did what Jo said, because she was older, but Lily had her way as well.

"If we play tea parties," she would say, "I can be a Pirate Captain who comes to tea." Jo would sigh and agree. She even let Lily wear her eye-patch, because fighting with her sister could just go on and on, and then there was no time for the game.

For the next few weeks, Jo was busy practising her mouse-dance all the time.

"Show me the battle steps," said Lily. "I like battles. Will you have a sword?"

"Yes," said Jo. "A sword or a stick."

"I hope you have a sword," said Lily. "Will you let me play with it a bit? Can you bring it home?"

"I shouldn't think so," said Jo. "All the swords will be kept in Miss Warne's cupboard, I expect."

"I wouldn't mind being a mouse," said Lily. "Especially if I could fight. Show me what you have to do in the battle and I'll do it with you."

"We haven't got the music," said Jo.

"Doesn't matter. You can
borrow my pirate's cutlass for a
sword if you like. I'll be a mouse,
too. You show me what you have
to do."

Jo showed Lily the steps of the
dance. Lily enjoyed creeping. She
liked waving her coathanger-
sword above her head, too, but
best of all was running very
quickly across the room on
tiptoe. She bumped into a corner
of Jo's doll's house and sent a
doll-sized teapot flying across the
floor. Then, when she was

stepping backwards, she
accidentally put her foot on one
of Nibbles the Rabbit's furry,
squashy ears.

"I shan't let you practise with
me," said Jo, "if you keep
bumping into everything."

"I won't any more," said Lily.
"It's fun being a mouse. Let's do
the dance again."

Chapter Three

One day, when Jo and Lily were alone together, Jo said, "I'll tell you a secret."

"What?"

"I wish I didn't have to wear a mouse-suit," said Jo. "I wish I could be a snowflake. They're wearing short white tutus and

sparkles on their hair."

"You were happy to be a mouse," said Lily, "at the beginning. You were happy when Miss Warne chose you."

"I *am* happy. Of course I am," said Jo. "Only I wish I was in the next class. They're being the snowflakes."

"Maybe you can be a snowflake another time."

Jo still looked glum.

Lily said, "I'm sure you'll be a very pretty mouse."

But whatever her sister said, Jo went on worrying about her mouse-costume.

"I want pink satin for the insides of my ears," she told her mum. "Bonny and Shenaz have both got pink satin. Their mums bought it in the market."

The tails were made from strips of soft, grey felt.

"Where can I get some?" Mum said. Luckily, Michelle had more than she needed, and Michelle's mum said Jo could have the spare bit.

"It's too short," said Jo, looking sideways in the mirror.

"No, it's not," said Mum firmly. "It's just right. Mice don't have very long tails, you know."

"Will it all be ready for next
week?" Jo asked.

"I hope so," said Mum. The sofa
was covered in funnily-shaped
pieces of pale grey fur fabric.

"Lily," Jo asked, "will you come to the class on Tuesday, just to see if the costume looks all right?"

Lily thought of snorting and saying 'no', but she, too, was longing to see all the costumes being tried on, so she smiled and said 'yes' instead.

"Wonders will never cease,"
said Mum. "Now, come over
here, Jo, and stick your arm out
so that I can see how long this
sleeve should be."

Lily took her drawing-pad to the
dancing class.
"I might feel like drawing some
of the mice," she said. "I like
drawing."

Everyone who was a mouse
had to parade across the floor for
Miss Warne to look at. Bonny's
mouse-ears were a little floppy
and needed extra stiffening, and
Michelle's grey tights were a bit
too dark, and Meg's sleeves

needed shortening, but Miss
Warne said nothing about Jo's tail,
even though it was much shorter
than all the others.

After everyone had changed
back into their pink leotards, Miss
Warne made an announcement:

"From now on, girls and boys, we'll be having our lessons at the High School, so that you can get used to the stage before the display. And I've got a lovely surprise for you all. Amy's little sister, Judy, who is only five and a half, has agreed to be the Fairy at the top of the Christmas tree for us. Isn't that wonderful? I'm sure she'll look absolutely sweet."

Chapter Four

"I'd hate to look absolutely sweet," said Lily, after the class, as they were walking back to Michelle's house. "I'm glad it's not me who has to be a Fairy. I didn't know there was a Fairy. You never said there was. Will she have to stand very still?"

"You never stop asking questions, do you?" said Jo. "I don't know what the Fairy has to do. I didn't know we were going to have a person at the top of the tree. I thought Miss Warne was going to put a doll up there."

"I know about the tree," said

Michelle, "because I've seen *The Nutcracker*. The Christmas tree gets enormous. It's magic. It grows and grows. It's much bigger than Clara and the Nutcracker."

"How is Miss Warne going to get a huge tree?" Lily asked.

"I don't know," said Jo and Michelle together.

"And how is Amy's little sister going to get to the top of the tree?"

Jo and Michelle cried, "We've told you already. We don't know. So just shush."

Lily found out about the
Christmas tree in the end. Jo told
her after the class at the High
School.

"It's clever," she said. "There's
this huge, huge triangle made out
of plywood and painted to look
like a Christmas tree. They've
even painted on the decorations.
Then, behind the triangle,
Melanie's dad has built a
platform. No-one can see it from
the front. Judy's going to stand up
there and try not to move. It will
look as if she's right at the top of
the tree."

"What a good idea," said Lily. "Can I come with you again and see it?"

"I suppose so," said Jo. "We'll ask Mum. It's the Dress Rehearsal next week. You can see all the costumes."

Mum said, "I don't see why you can't go, Lily. If you'd like to, and if Miss Warne doesn't mind. But I thought you said ballet class was boring."

"I want to see the tree," Lily said. "I want to see the Fairy."

"Right," said Mum. "I'll come and pick you up from the High School after the Dress Rehearsal."

Lily packed her drawing-pad and her crayons in her school bag. She would draw a picture of the Christmas tree, she thought, with a real, live fairy at the top of it.

Chapter Five

"Ssh, children," said Miss Warne at the beginning of the class.

"I'm afraid I've got a piece of very disappointing news for you. Little Judy, who was going to be our Fairy, has just come down with chickenpox."

There were gasps and sighs from all around the hall. Even Lily stopped gazing at the Christmas tree and looked at Miss Warne instead.

"It's such a pity," she went on.
"Judy would have put the
finishing touch to our display.
And I brought the Fairy costume
along to show you all. Look, this
is the dress."

Miss Warne opened a big plastic
carrier bag and took out

the Fairy dress. Everyone except
Lily said: "Ooh", and "Aah".
Their eyes opened wide. Never in
all the world had there ever been a
dress as beautiful as this one. It
was made of a silky material. It
had huge, puffy sleeves. It was very
pale pink. The skirt stuck out,
because of all the deeper pink
petticoats under it. Someone had
sewn pearls and sequins all over it.
They caught the light and dazzled
everyone. No-one said a word,
and then Jo put her hand up.

"Please, Miss
Warne," she said.
"I've got a sister.
She's over there.
She could be the
Fairy."

Everyone in the High School hall turned to look at Lily.

"Come down to the front, dear," said Miss Warne, "and let's have a look at you."

Lily blushed.

"Hhmm," said Miss Warne. "I think it will fit... would you like to go and try it on for me? You go with her, Jo."

In the cloakroom, Lily started moaning.

"Why did you say I'd be the Fairy? I *hate* dresses like this. I don't want to do it. I won't do it..."

"You *will* do it," said Jo. "You must do it. The whole show will be spoiled if you don't."

"Hasn't anyone else got a sister?" Lily pleaded.

"Everyone else's sisters are too young or too old. You're just right. See how nice you look!"

"I don't look nice. I look stupid."

"Come on," said Jo. "We'll go and show Miss Warne. She'll decide."

Miss Warne decided that Lily looked very pretty.

"So that's that," Jo said. "You're the Fairy now."

In bed that night, Lily heard a funny noise.

"Jo, are you crying?"

"Go to sleep."

"What's the matter?"

"Nothing," said Jo. "I just wish *I* could be the Fairy and wear that lovely dress."

"Jo, I've had an idea," Lily said. "Can I climb down and tell you?"

"OK." Lily clambered down to the bottom bunk. She whispered in Jo's ear.

"Will it work?" Jo asked. "Do you think it will?"

"Yes," said Lily. "I know it will."

Jo was so happy that she kissed her little sister on the cheek.

"There's no need to be soppy," said Lily. "I'm going back to bed now."

Chapter Six

The curtains opened, and there was the enormous Christmas tree with a beautiful Fairy right at the top of it. Everyone started clapping.

"Look!" said Michelle's mum. "Is that your Lily?"

"Yes, of course it is," said Lily's mum, and then she looked again and said, "No, it's not... it's Jo... it was meant to be Lily. Whatever can have happened?"

"Jo looks beautiful, though, doesn't she?" said Michelle's mum.

Jo, standing on the platform behind the painted tree, was very frightened. She was also very happy. This dress, she thought, is the best dress in the world and I'm wearing it. When, she wondered, would Miss Warne notice? At the moment she was busy doing up mouse-costumes at the side of the stage.

Lily had said, "Maybe she won't notice at all. Just turn away a bit and she might not see your face."

Jo remembered this and turned a little to her left. Now she couldn't see Lily in her mouse-costume, with all the other mice.

When the battle began, though,

Jo knew at once which mouse was her sister. She was the one with the shortest tail of all. It didn't matter. Lily hadn't forgotten a single step that Jo had taught her, and she waved her sword better than any of the others.

In the audience, Michelle's mum said, "Look! I think that's your Lily... with the short tail."

"Goodness," said Lily's mum. "The naughty girls... they've swapped parts. I *knew* Lily would never agree to wear a dress like that."

Miss Warne *did* notice, after all.

"I should be cross," she told Jo and Lily after the show was over, "but I can't be. You were the perfect Fairy, Jo, and Lily, I don't think I've ever in my life seen a fiercer or mousier mouse! Why don't you come to ballet class, like your sister?"

"No thank you, Miss Warne," said Lily. "I'm going to ask my mum if I can do judo."

THE END